Men Love Football

Women Love Foreplay

(And Other Crazy Comparisons)

by
IAN COHEN
&
SEAN COLLINS

CCC PUBLICATIONS

Published by

CCC Publications
9725 Lurline Avenue
Chatsworth CA 91311

Copyright © 2000 Ian Cohen & Sean Collins

All rights reserved by CCC Publications. No part of this book may be reproduced or transmitted in any form or by any means, electronic or mechanical, including photocopying, recording or by any information storage and retrieval system, without the written permission of the publisher, except where permitted by law. For information address: CCC Publications; 9725 Lurline Avenue; Chatsworth, CA 91311.

Manufactured in the United States of America

Cover © 2000 CCC Publications

Interior illustrations © 2000 CCC Publications

Cover & interior illustrations by Adrian Barrios

Original cover concept by Joel Ferris

Cover/Interior production by
Continental Imaging Center, Chatsworth, CA

ISBN: 1-57644-114-8

If your local U.S. bookstore is out of stock, copies of this book may be obtained by mailing check or money order for $6.99 per book (plus $2.75 to cover postage and handling) to:
CCC Publications;
9725 Lurline Avenue
Chatsworth, CA 91311.

Pre-publication Edition – 05/00

❧ DEDICATION ❧

It takes an abnormal childhood to develop a true sense of humor. This book is therefore dedicated to my parents, Sidney and Dallas.

Special thanks to Kristina, Carol and Buchin; two saints and one sick bastard who helped make this book possible (on second thought, make that one saint and two sick bastards).

– Ian Cohen

It wasn't an abnormal childhood, but perhaps the glue I sniffed throughout second grade that shaped my sense of humor.

This book is therefore dedicated to that glue and all those who have made me laugh, especially my parents, Jack and Maryann, sister Victoria, brother Stephen, as well as firearms specialist Voodoo Kincaid and beautiful Gerri Jo.

– Sean Collins

INTRODUCTION

After failing repeatedly to sell any screenplays to the major Hollywood studios, we shifted gears and sought alternate means to gain recognition for our comedic writing talents. Unfortunately, television, radio, music, newspaper and community theater executives wouldn't return our calls either.

Before throwing in the towel and donning our Taco Bell uniforms, we gave the fine people in the mass media one last chance to reap the rewards of our literary prowess, by writing a book that could really make an impact... or a quick profit.

Deciding to steer clear of topics we knew absolutely nothing about, like helping people with their problems, we settled on a theme that was sure to touch 'most everyone's funny bone—comparing the differences that exist between human beings from all walks of life. Let's face it, there are few things more entertaining than watching a couple of folks from opposite sides of the track caught up in a heated debate. With this in mind, we spent one painstaking year comparing how specific groups of people embrace life so differently. We then spent an additional year coming up with the title, "Men Love Football, Women Love Foreplay."

And while the majority of our work concentrates on comparing the opposing views of men and women, you'll find a healthy portion focuses on the different mindsets of those who are: *married & single; white collar & white trash; straight & gay; Irish & Italian; baby boomers & gen-Xers;* and *New Yorkers & Californians,* just to name a few.

As with most authors, it is our goal to enlighten, educate and entertain. However, we'd be kidding ourselves if we expected to accomplish all three. Hell, even two is highly unlikely. It is therefore our hope that if we can just make most people laugh out loud while reading this book, it will all have been worth it.

Enjoy!

Ian Cohen and Sean Collins

Most Proud Of
Women

FINDING THEIR SOUL MATE

THEIR HAIR LENGTH

THE WEIGHT THEY LOST

THE MAN THEY CAUGHT

SHOPPING CONQUESTS

EXTENSIVE WARDROBE

QUALITY OF PARTNERS

FAVORITE SOAP OPERA

HUSBAND'S CHARM

PERFUMES

GARDEN

Most Proud Of
MEN

→ LOSING THEIR VIRGINITY

→ THEIR PENIS LENGTH

→ THE MUSCLE THEY GAINED

→ THE FISH THEY CAUGHT

→ SEXUAL CONQUESTS

→ FAVORITE 12 YEAR OLD GRAY T-SHIRT

→ QUANTITY OF PARTNERS

→ FAVORITE SPORTS TEAM

→ WIFE'S BREASTS

→ FARTS

→ SEATS AT MADISON SQUARE GARDEN

Things To Look Forward To In Life
Women

FIRST KISS

GETTING PROPOSED TO

WEDDING DAY

ANNUAL NORDSTROM SHOE SALE

STARTING A FAMILY

FINDING A SOPHISTICATED, CARING, WEALTHY GENTLEMAN WHO LISTENS

Things To Look Forward To In Life

MEN

→ **FIRST CAR**

→ **GETTING TO 3RD BASE**

→ **OPENING DAY (ANY SPORT)**

→ **ANNUAL SPORT'S ILLUSTRATED SWIMSUIT EDITION**

→ **STARTING A PROJECT IN THE GARAGE**

→ **FINDING A FREE SPIRITED 19 YEAR OLD COLLEGE STUDENT, LOOKING TO SHACK UP WITH A FORTY-SOMETHING DIVORCEE**

Foreplay Preferences
Women

SOFT KISSES

WARM HUGS

SENSUOUS MASSAGE

EAR NIBBLING

TICKLING

FANTASY ROLE PLAYING

SEXY WHISPERS

SEDUCTIVE STRIPPING

READING EROTIC LITERATURE

EATING SENSUOUS FRUIT OFF BODY

SPOONING

FOOT RUBS

CUDDLING

CARESSING

Foreplay Preferences
MEN

Worst Things to Hear from The Opposite Sex

MEN (Don't Want To Hear)

"I USED TO BE A MAN."

"DON'T FEEL BAD, IT HAPPENS TO LOTS OF GUYS."

"MY MOTHER WILL BE STAYING WITH US FOR A WHILE."

"IT'S OK, **I** DON'T NEED TO HAVE AN ORGASM."

"IS IT IN YET?"

"I MAKE DOUBLE YOUR SALARY."

"YOU WANT **ME** TO PUT **WHAT** IN MY MOUTH?"

"OH YES, MARK, DON'T STOP!" (Your name is Larry, your brother's name is Mark)

Worst Things to Hear from The Opposite Sex
Women (Don't want to hear)

"ARE YOU STILL DIETING?"

"YOUR FRIEND SHEILA HAS IMPLANTS AND SHE LOOKS FANTASTIC!"

"IS IT ME OR IS YOUR ASS GETTING A LITTLE BIGGER?"

"MY MOTHER WILL BE STAYING WITH US FOR A WHILE."

"I'M JUST THANKFUL MY GENITAL HERPES IS DORMANT."

"I CAN LAST A FULL 3 MINUTES."

"HEY, SOME GUYS ARE INTO FAT CHICKS."

OH YES, MARK DON'T STOP!" (Your name is Carol, your gay neighbor's name is Mark)

Preferred Things To Do After Orgasm
Women

HAVE ANOTHER ONE

CUDDLE

TALK ABOUT HOW WONDERFUL IT WAS

CARESS EACH OTHER

SHOWER TOGETHER

MAKE LOVE AGAIN

SMOKE IN BED

LATE NIGHT STROLL

FIND THE DRY SPOT

Preferred Things To Do After Orgasm
MEN

→ **SLEEP**

→ **MAKE A SANDWICH**

→ **WATCH SPORTSCENTER**

→ **GO HOME**

→ **SHOWER ALONE**

→ **MAKE ANOTHER SANDWICH**

→ **SMOKE ON THE WAY HOME**

→ **PAY AND GET OUT**

→ **FIND THE DRY SPOT**

Vacation Entertainment

Women

WATCH THE SUNSET

SIGHTSEEING TOURS

SHOP

SLOW DANCE UNDER THE STARS

MASSAGE, FACIAL, MANICURE AND SEAWEED WRAP AT HOTEL SPA

ENJOY A FROZEN COCKTAIL BY THE POOL

TRY TO LEARN NEW CULTURES OF THE NATIVES

Vacation Entertainment
MEN

→ **WATCH ESPN**

→ **PAY PER VIEW**

→ **SLEEP**

→ **LAP DANCES AT TOPLESS BARS**

→ **CRAPS, BLACKJACK, POKER AND SPORTS BETTING AT HOTEL CASINO**

→ **ENJOY A BEER BY THE TV**

→ **TRY TO SLEEP WITH THE NATIVES**

Things To Say When You're In Love
Women

I LOVE YOU.

I WANT YOU TO BE MY FIRST.

I'D DIE WITHOUT YOU.

YOU'RE MY SOUL MATE.

YOU COMPLETE ME.

YOU ARE MY WORLD.

I WANT TO HAVE YOUR CHILDREN.

I WANT TO SPEND THE REST OF MY LIFE WITH YOU.

YOU MEAN EVERYTHING TO ME.

I GIVE YOU MY HEART.

I AM TRULY BLESSED TO HAVE FOUND YOU.

Things To Say When You're In Love
MEN

"DITTO"

Favorite Things To See In A Movie
Women

LOVERS
CROSSING PATHS

BRAD PITT'S
SMILE

ARNOLD SCHWARZENEGGER'S
PECS

MEL GIBSON'S
BUTT

DISCOVERING
ROMANCE
IN PARIS

WOMEN BONDING

Favorite Things To See In A Movie

MEN

→ SHARON STONE
UNCROSSING HER LEGS

→ BRAD PITT'S SMILE AS A
BULLET DRILLS HIS HEAD

→ JENNIFER LOVE HEWITT'S
BREASTS

→ MEL GIBSON
HEAD-BUTTING SOMEONE

→ DISCOVERING THE
RED LIGHT DISTRICT
IN AMSTERDAM

→ WOMEN BONDING
IN THE NUDE

Qualities Sought In A Mate
Women

INTELLIGENCE

SENSE OF HUMOR

HONESTY

GENEROSITY

WEALTH

PASSION

MASCULINITY

PATIENCE

AFFECTIONATE

COMPASSION

CREATIVITY

KINDNESS

DEPENDABILITY

Qualities Sought In A Mate
MEN

Big Rack

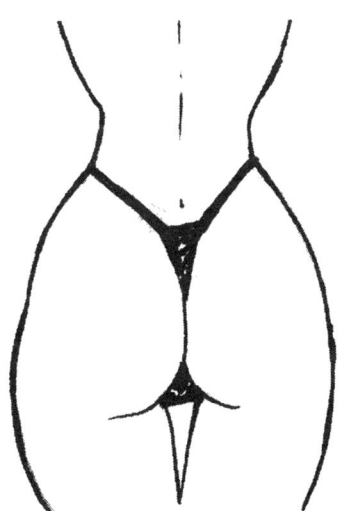

Great Ass

Common Little Fibs

Women

THAT WAS THE BEST SEX I EVER HAD!

I'VE NEVER DONE THAT BEFORE.

I'VE NEVER HAD A ONE NIGHT STAND.

I DON'T MIND WATCHING THE ENTIRE GAME.

POKER WITH THE GUYS SOUNDS LIKE FUN!

I'M SURE I'LL LIKE WHATEVER YOU ORDER.

YOUR MOM IS VERY SWEET.

YOUR THE ONLY GUY I'VE EVER HAD ANAL SEX WITH.

THEY'RE REAL.

YOU'RE SO MUCH BETTER AT THAT THAN MY LAST BOYFRIEND.

OF COURSE I CAME.

HE'S JUST A FRIEND.

Common Little Fibs

MEN

YOU'RE ONE OF THE FEW WOMEN WHO LOOKS GOOD WITHOUT MAKEUP.

BIG BREASTS REALLY AREN'T THAT IMPORTANT TO ME.

NO, REALLY, I DON'T MIND WHEN YOUR PARENTS COME OVER UNANNOUNCED.

I THINK A LITTLE EXTRA FEW POUNDS MAKES YOU LOOK CUTER.

SURE, I'D LIKE TO SPEND THE DAY SHOPPING WITH YOU.

WOW, I'VE NEVER DONE THAT WITH A WOMAN BEFORE.

YOU <u>DON'T</u> LOOK FAT IN THAT DRESS.

I'D RATHER BE WITH YOU THAN ANY OF THOSE VICTORIA'S SECRET MODELS.

SHE'S JUST A FRIEND.

3 Granted Wishes

Women

1. A BODY LIKE PAMELA ANDERSON

2. A FAIRY TALE WEDDING

3. AN UNLIMITED EXPENSE ACCOUNT AT THE STORE OF HER CHOICE

3 Granted Wishes

MEN

1. SEX WITH PAMELA ANDERSON

2. SEX WITH JENNIFER ANISTON

3. SEX WITH PAMELA ANDERSON AND JENNIFER ANISTON WHILE ALL HIS FRIENDS FROM HIGH SCHOOL WATCH

Products Found In The Shower

Women

5 KINDS OF SHAMPOO
4 KINDS OF CONDITIONER
6 DIFFERENT SCENTED BODY SOAPS
3 DIFFERENT EXFOLIATORS
MAKE-UP REMOVER
PUMICE STONE
2 BODY LOOFAHS
SOAP PUFF THING
3 TYPES OF BODY OIL
BACK BRUSH
SHAVING CREAM
RAZORS
OTHER HAIR REMOVAL PRODUCTS
SHOWER MASSAGER (ABLE TO REACH DIFFICULT PLACES)
FACE SCRUBBER GLOVE
SCENTED CANDLES
DOUCHE
WASHCLOTH
BATH PILLOW
RADIO
COMB

Products Found In The Shower
MEN

BAR OF SOAP

EMPTY BOTTLE OF SHAMPOO

Website Preferences

Women

WWW.BARGAINS.COM

WWW.HEADGAMES.COM

WWW.SHOES.COM

WWW.MENAREBASTARDS.COM

WWW.MAKEOVERS.COM

WWW.MEANDMYCAT.COM

WWW.LANDINGARICHMAN.COM

WWW.ALIMONY.COM

WWW.GEORGECLOONEY.COM

WWW.MULTIPLEORGASMS.COM

Website Preferences
MEN

WWW.COLLEGECHEERLEADERS.COM

WWW.LESBIANS.COM

WWW.SCOREBOARD.COM

WWW.FANTASYSLUTS.COM

WWW.BEER.COM

WWW.KINKYGIRLS.COM

WWW.HORNYHOUSEWIVES.COM

WWW.CHEAPHOOKERS.COM

WWW.WOMENWHOLIKENERDS.COM

WWW.ORALANNIE.COM

Kitchen Accessories
Single Woman

SPICE RACK
FOOD PROCESSOR
SALAD SPINNER
BLENDER
GARLIC PRESS
CHEESE GRATER
CARROT PEELER
ROLLING PIN
MIXER
COLANDER
MINI CHOPPER
16-PC. STAINLESS STEEL COOKWARE
12-PC. CUTLERY SET
CHINA SET
MICROWAVE
CAPPUCCINO MAKER
COFFEE GRINDER
TOASTER OVEN
NON-STICK PANS
WIRE WHISK
MEASURING CUPS & SPOONS
VEGI-STEAMER
FONDUE SET
PIE TINS
SOUP TUREEN
BAKE PANS
GLASSWARE

Kitchen Accessories
SINGLE MAN

MICROWAVE
CAN OPENER
BOWL FOR CEREAL
SWISS ARMY KNIFE
POT
FREE FOOTBALL GLASS
FROM GAS STATION
(WITH FILL-UP)

Speed Dial Listings
MARRIED MAN

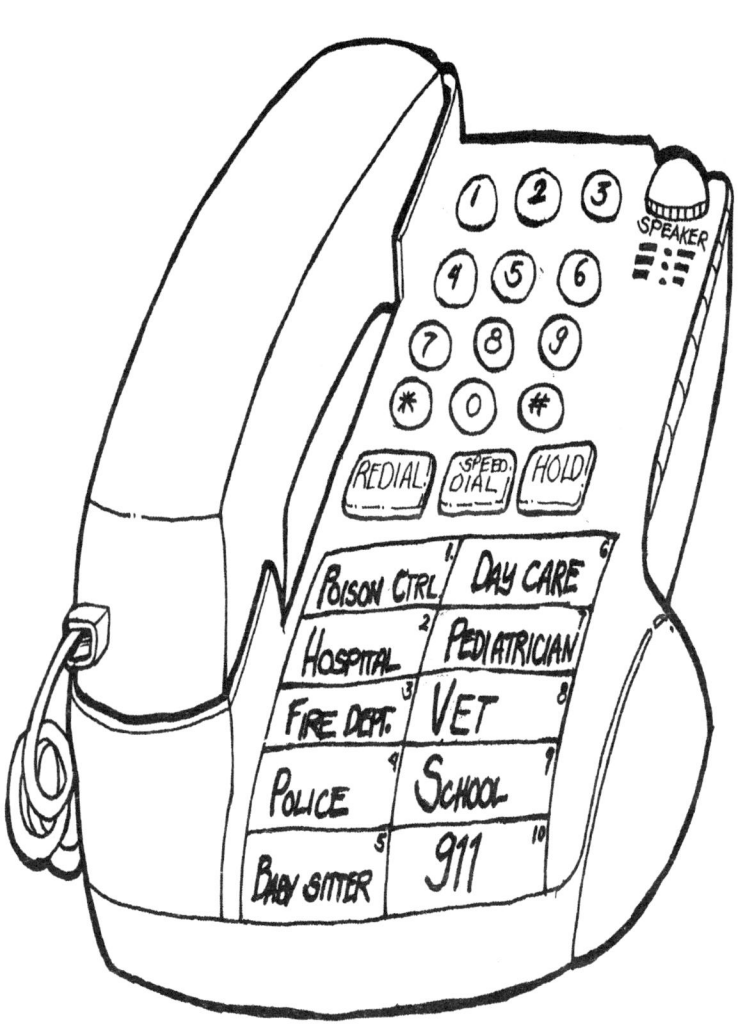

Speed Dial Listings
BACHELOR

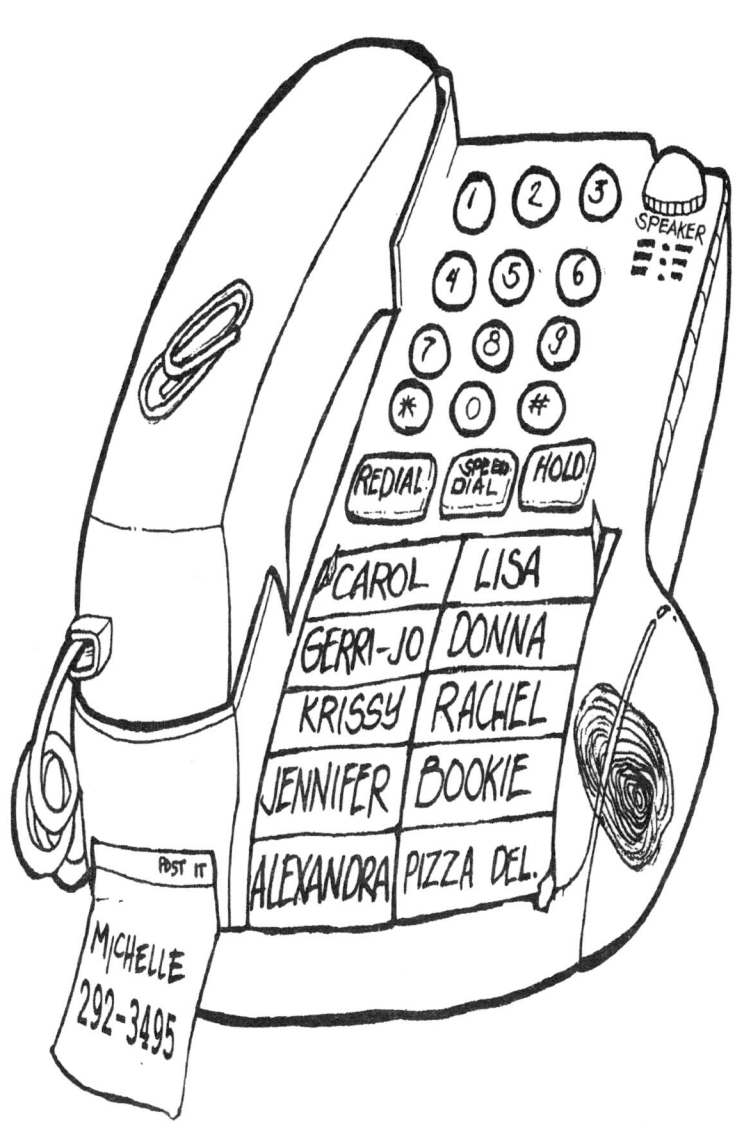

29

Sources Of Nutrition
Single Woman

BERRIES, PEACHES, GRAPES, PLUMS	*Fruit*
APPLES	*Fiber*
CORN	*Starch*
OATBRAN	*Grains*
NUTS	*Proteins*
MILK	*Calcium*
CARROTS	*Vitamin A*
ORANGE JUICE	*Vitamin C*

Sources Of Nutrition
SINGLE MAN

Fruit	**FRUITLOOPS**
Fiber	**APPLEJACKS**
Starch	**CORN FLAKES**
Grains	**BEER**
Proteins	**BEERNUTS**
Calcium	**MILK DUDS**
Vitamin A	**CARROT CAKE**
Vitamin C	**ORANGE JUICE WITH VODKA**

An Evening Of Passion
NEWLYWEDS

PUT ON YOUR SEXIEST OUTFIT

WEAR FAVORITE COLOGNE/PERFUME

BUY PRETTY FLOWERS

PLAY SOFT ROMANTIC MUSIC

PREPARE A ROMANTIC DINNER

LIGHT SOME CANDLES

DIM THE LIGHTS

SET UP WARM BUBBLE BATH

POSITION MASSAGE OIL NEXT TO BED

BRING OUT FAVORITE ADULT TOYS AND READING MATERIAL

SLOWLY UNDRESS EACH OTHER

TAKE TIME TO EXPLORE EVERY INCH OF YOUR PARTNER'S BODY

ESTIMATED TIME: 3 HOURS

An Evening Of Passion
MARRIED WITH CHILDREN

GET RID OF KIDS

TAKE OFF YOUR OWN CLOTHES

SKIP THE FOREPLAY

QUICKLY DO IT BEFORE SOMETHING CAN GO WRONG

ESTIMATED TIME: 3 MINUTES

Cleaning Products
Women

PLEDGE
WINDEX
LYSOL
TILE-X
409
HANDY WIPES
CARPET CLEANER
SPOT REMOVER
BLEACH
AMMONIA
PALMOLIVE
SOS PADS
PAPER TOWELS
CLOROX 2
X14 SOAP SCUM REMOVER
DISSOLVIT
DAWN
ELECTROSOL
TIDE
WISK
ANTI-BACTERIAL DISINFECTANT

Cleaning Products

MEN

WATER

TOILET PAPER

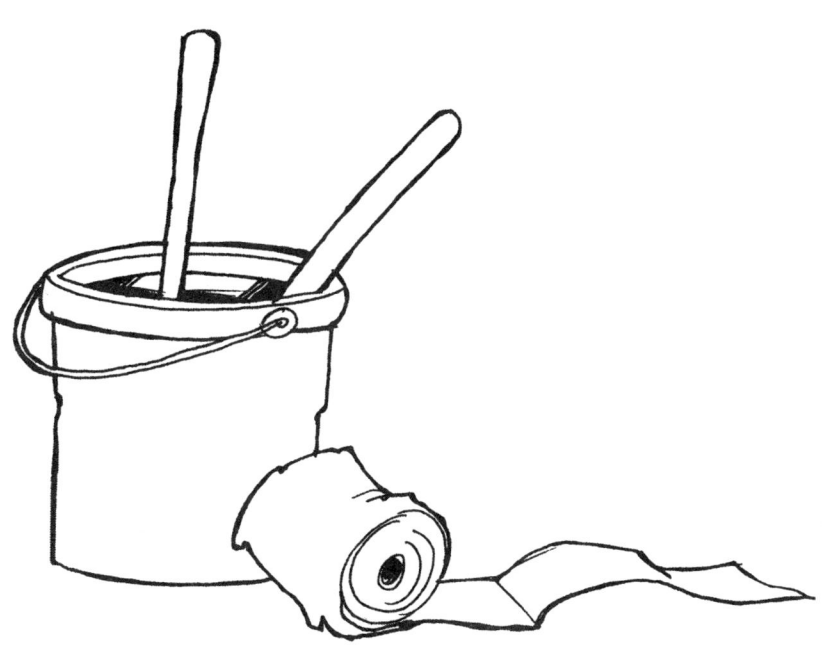

Adult Movie Preferences
Women

FRENCH ESCAPADES

SECRET DESIRES

MOONLIGHT KISSES

LADY CHATTERLY'S LOVER

SWEET SEDUCTIONS

FRIENDS AND LOVERS

NOTHING BUT FANTASIES

A STEAMY ENCOUNTER

Adult Movie Preferences
MEN

→ **SLUTS OF BULGARIA**

→ **PRISON GIRL SECRETS**

→ **NYMPHS FROM MARS**

→ **LADY CHATTERLY'S DONKEY**

→ **SIX CHICKS AND A MIDGET**

→ **PIMPS AND HOOKERS**

→ **NOTHING BUT D-CUPS**

→ **3 WOMEN AND A SHAVING KIT**

Advantages

Small-Breasted Women

WON'T
SAG

MEN WILL APPRECIATE YOUR
CONVERSATION SKILLS

EASIER TO
TURN OVER IN BED

CHANCE OF
SEXUAL HARRASSMENT
DECLINES 50%

ESTABLISH FREQUENT EYE CONTACT

BETTER CHANCE OF
BECOMING A RUNWAY MODEL

EXCEL IN GYMNASTIC
COMPETITION

EASIER TO BOUNCE ON A
TRAMPOLINE WITHOUT
GETTING INJURED

FULFILL DREAMS OF BECOMING
A BALLET DANCER

Advantages

Large-Breasted Women

→ HELPS GET INTO S.A.G. (SCREEN ACTOR'S GUILD)

→ MEN WILL APPRECIATE YOUR CONVERSATION PIECES

→ EASIER TO GET MEN TO TURN OVER THEIR WALLETS

→ CHANCES FOR WINNING A SEXUAL HARRASSMENT LAWSUIT INCREASE 50%

→ AVOID PRE-NUP CONTRACT

→ BETTER CHANCE OF BECOMING A BUDWEISER GIRL

→ EXCEL IN WET T-SHIRT CONTESTS

→ EASIER TO BOUNCE A CHECK AND GET AWAY WITH IT

→ FULFILL DREAMS OF BECOMING A GO-GO DANCER

How We Misbehave
DOGS

- SEX WITH ANY FEMALE WHO COMES ALONG
- DON'T CLEAN UP AFTER THEMSELVES
- DRINK OUT OF THE TOILET
- CONSTANT BEGGING
- MOUNTING THE NEIGHBOR'S LEG
- URINATING IN THE FLOWER-BED
- SNIFFING A STRANGE CROTCH
- DON'T LISTEN
- CAN'T STAY STILL LONG ENOUGH
- CURL UP AND SLEEP AFTER SEX
- CONSTANTLY LICKING THEMSELVES

How We Misbehave
GUYS

→ SEX WITH ANY FEMALE WHO COMES ALONG

→ DON'T CLEAN UP AFTER THEMSELVES

→ DRINK OUT OF THE CARTON

→ CONSTANT BEGGING

→ MOUNTING THE NEIGHBOR'S WIFE

→ URINATING IN THE FLOWER-BED

→ SNIFFING A STRANGE CROTCH

→ DON'T LISTEN

→ CAN'T STAY HARD LONG ENOUGH

→ ROLL OVER AND SLEEP AFTER SEX

→ CONSTANTLY PLAYING WITH THEMSELVES

Family Activities
Good Parenting

FEEDING THE DUCKS

A DAY AT THE BALLPARK

GAMES WITH THE WATER SPRINKLER

THE EGG TOSS

AFTERNOON ROLLERCOASTER RIDES

KITE FLYING ON A BREEZY DAY

PTA MEETING

ANNUAL PILGRIMAGE TO HOLY LAND

CARIBBEAN GETAWAY

REMOVING LITTER FROM THE NEIGHBORHOOD

STUFFING PRESENTS INTO THE CHRISTMAS STOCKINGS

BROADWAY SHOW

Family Activities

Bad Parenting

→ FEEDING THE SLOT MACHINES

→ A DAY AT THE OTB

→ GAMES WITH THE GARBAGE DISPOSAL

→ THE SCISSOR TOSS

→ MIDNIGHT SUBWAY RIDES

→ KITE FLYING DURING AN ELECTRICAL STORM

→ KLAN MEETING

→ ANNUAL PILGRIMAGE TO NEVADA BROTHEL

→ KOSOVO GETAWAY

→ REMOVING ASBESTOS FROM A CONDEMEND BUILDING

→ STUFFING TWENTIES INTO A STRIPPER'S STOCKINGS

→ PEEP SHOW

Favorite Movies
Straight

ROCKY

DIE HARD

TERMINATOR

DIRTY HARRY

THE BIRDS

BATMAN

DEEP THROAT

GOODFELLAS

ESCAPE FROM NEW YORK

THE POPE OF GREENWICH VILLAGE

STAR WARS

Favorite Movies

Gays

→ **ROCKY HORROR PICTURE SHOW**

→ **DIE HARD** (Not the Bruce Willis movie)

→ **TERMS OF ENDEARMENT**

→ **DIRTY DANCING**

→ **BIRDCAGE**

→ **ZORRO (THE GAY BLADE)**

→ **DEEP IMPACT**
(Not the Morgan Freeman film)

→ **REALLY GOOD FELLAS**

→ **ESCAPE FROM WITCH MOUNTAIN**

→ **THE WIZARD OF OZ**

→ **A STAR IS BORN**

TV Shows We'd Like To See
Straight

WHORES SAY THE
FUNNIEST THINGS

TOUCHED BY A
PORN STAR

BAYWATCH 2

EVERYBODY LOVES RACHEL

THE X-RATED FILES

60 MINUTES...
OF NAKED BABES

WHOSE BREASTS ARE
THEY ANYWAY?

PARTY OF FIVE PLAYMATES

I DREAM OF JEANNIE
ON TOP OF ME

THE BARELY LEGAL BUNCH

TV Shows We'd Like To See
Gays

SUDDENLY SUSAN'S BROTHER

TOUCHED BY A LARGE BLACK MAN

GAYWATCH

EVERYBODY LOVES RAMONE

SAN FRANCISCO 91690

2 GUYS, ANOTHER GUY AND A PIZZA PLACE

MURRAY LOVES CHACHI

MY 3 NEPHEWS

C.H.I.P.S.—THE NEXT GENERATION

GILLIGAN'S ALL-MALE ISLAND

Favorite Sports Teams
Straight

STEELERS — *Football*

LIGHTNING — *Hockey*

YANKEES — *Baseball*

BULLS — *Basketball*

WILDCATS — *College*

Favorite Sports Teams

Gays

Football	*Packers*
Hockey	*Flames*
Baseball	*Blue Jays*
Basketball	*Jazz*
College	*Gamecocks*

Last Will And Testament
Yuppie

I hereby bequeath the following possessions to my lovely wife Julia, and two children, Andrew and Victoria...

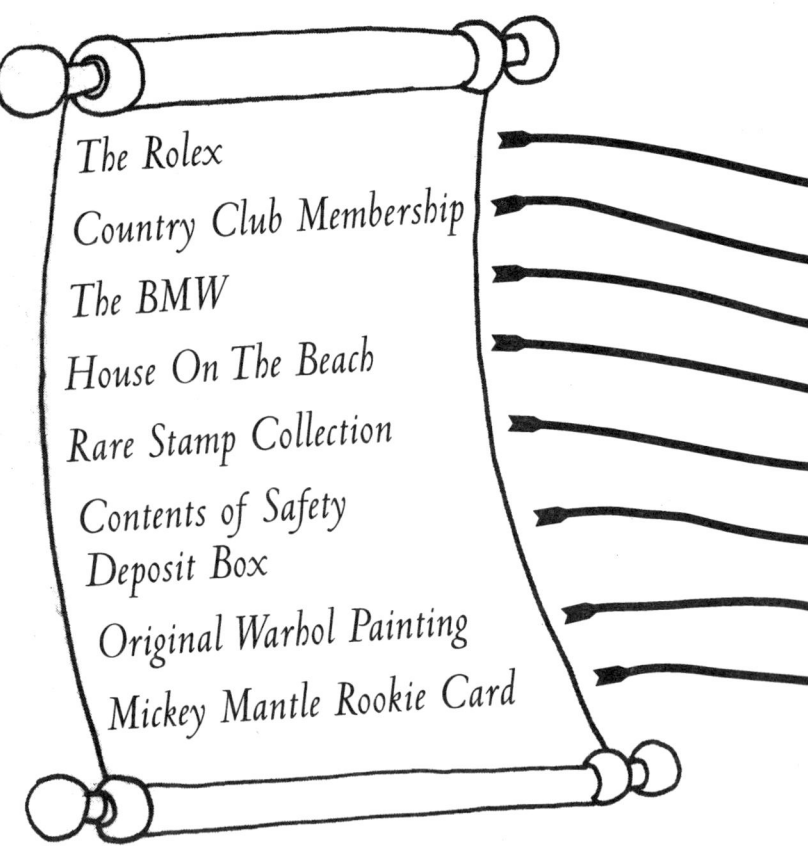

- The Rolex
- Country Club Membership
- The BMW
- House On The Beach
- Rare Stamp Collection
- Contents of Safety Deposit Box
- Original Warhol Painting
- Mickey Mantle Rookie Card

Last Will And Testament
Yokel

Let my old lady and the 12 younguns split this stuff up now that I'm 6 ft. in the ground...

THe TiMex
elks CluB meMbership
thE RV
outHouse in The back
fooD Stamp colleection
The tackle Box CoNtEnts
the PoKer plaYing dogs PaiNTing
WalmArt card
BAR 69 charge

51

Today's "IN" Names For A Baby
Yuppies

DAKOTA

HARRISON

TYLER

BLAKE

KAITLYN

HUNTER

BRITTNEY

MONTANA

SKYLER

DESTINY

Today's "IN" Names For A Baby
Yokels

CLEETUS

BUFORD

DAISY

VERN

LITTLE EARL

JUNIOR

JETHRO

CARL

LUCY

BILLY - (FOLLOWED BY ANY OTHER NAME)

Forms Of Relaxation
Yuppie

BURN INCENSE

YOGA

PETTING SOMETHING CUTE AND FURRY

SMOKING A JOINT

BEATING THE HEAVY BAG

LIGHTING CANDLES

SIPPING BRANDY

ACUPRESSURE

SAILING

CHARDONNAY BY THE FIREPLACE

PLAYING PIANO

REPOTTING A PLANT

Forms Of Relaxation
Yokel

→ **BURN RUBBER**

→ **YODEL**

→ **KILLING SOMETHING CUTE AND FURRY**

→ **CHEWING TOBACCO**

→ **BEATING THE KIDS**

→ **LIGHTING A CAMPFIRE**

→ **GUZZLING MOONSHINE**

→ **AMMUNITION RELOADING**

→ **WHITTLING**

→ **BEER BY THE TOOLSHED**

→ **PLAYING BANJO**

→ **REBUILDING AN ENGINE**

Musical Influences
Baby Boomers

- THE BEACH BOYS
- THE DOORS
- MAMAS AND PAPAS
- HENDRIX
- ELVIS PRESLEY
- GLADYS KNIGHT & THE PIPS
- GRATEFUL DEAD
- ALICE COOPER
- MANFRED MANN
- BREAD
- SIMON AND GARFUNKEL
- THE BEATLES
- 5 TOPS

Musical Influences
Gen-X

→ **THE BEASTIE BOYS**

→ **THE SPICE GIRLS**

→ **PUFF DADDY**

→ **HANSON**

→ **ELVIS COSTELLO**

→ **MARKY MARK & THE FUNKY BUNCH**

→ **DEAD PRESIDENTS**

→ **ALICE IN CHAINS**

→ **MARILYN MANSON**

→ **KORN**

→ **GUNS AND ROSES**

→ **RATT**

→ **9 INCH NAILS**

Song Titles
Baby Boomer

MY GIRL

WHAT'S GOING ON

LOVE ME
TWO TIMES

I WANNA HOLD YOUR HAND

SOUNDS OF
SILENCE

SATISFACTION

L.A. WOMAN

HEARD IT THROUGH THE
GRAPEVINE

PARSLEY, SAGE,
ROSEMARY & THYME

Song Titles
Gen-X (Urban)

→ MY GIRL'S A HO

→ WHAT'S UP MUTHAF'ER

→ PUNCH HER TWO TIMES, (THE BITCH HAS IT COMIN)

→ I WANNA KICK YOUR ASS

SOUNDS OF MY 9 MILLIMETER

→ MY HO DON'T GIVE ME NO SATISFACTION

→ COMPTON BITCHES

→ I HEARD YOU BEEN TALKIN SOME CRAP

→ HEROINE, CRACK, METH AND MALT LIQUOR

Sports Fan
Baby Boomer

Sports Fan
Gen-X

Parents' Greatest Fears
Jewish Parents

SON WON'T BECOME A DOCTOR

NO GRANDCHILDREN

CHILDREN MOVING OUT OF THE HOUSE THEY GREW UP IN

DAUGHTER GETTING PREGNANT BEFORE SHE'S MARRIED

DAUGHTER MARRIES A MAN WHO IS ALL WRONG FOR HER

CHILD CANNOT PASS THE BAR

DRUG DEALERS IN THE NEIGHBORHOOD

SUDDEN INFANT CRIB DEATH, CHILDREN'S LEUKEMIA, AUTOMOBILE ACCIDENT

PEDOPHILES

DAUGHTER WILL MARRY A BLACK MAN

Parents' Greatest Fears
REDNECK PARENTS

→ SON WON'T BECOME ELIGIBLE FOR PAROLE

→ **MORE GRANDCHILDREN**

→ CHILDREN STAYING IN THE TRAILER THEY GREW UP IN

→ **DAUGHTER GETTING PREGNANT BEFORE SHE'S 12**

→ DAUGHTER MARRIES A COUSIN WHO IS ALL WRONG FOR HER

→ **CHILD CANNOT PASS A BAR**

→ GATORS IN THE YARD

→ **RICKETS, RABIES, SCURVY, TICKS, COYOTES, & ANTI-FREEZE**

→ UNCLE HANK

→ **DAUGHTER WILL MARRY A BLACK MAN**

Recreation

GYM RAT

A RUN ON THE TREADMILL ▶

30 MINUTES OF SPIN CLASS ▶

60 MINUTES OF STAIRMASTER ▶

LIFT 40 LB. DUMBELLS

INCREASE WEIGHT ▶

STOMACH CRUNCHES ▶

LEG LIFTS ▶

CHANGE BARBELL PLATES ▶

ADJUST BENCH POSITION ▶

Recreation
Couch Potato

→ A RUN TO THE FRIDGE

→ 30 MINUTES OF SPIN CITY

→ 60 MINUTES

→ LIFT 12 OZ. BEVERAGE

→ INCREASE VOLUME

→ CAPTAIN CRUNCH

→ LIFTING LEG ONTO COFFEE TABLE

→ CHANGE CHANNEL

→ ADJUST RECLINER POSITION

Daily Gripes
CHECHNYA RESIDENTS

LACK OF FOOD

MAINTAINING
FIRM POSITIONS

SIGNING
PEACE ACCORDS

AIR RAIDS

NOT ENOUGH
AMBULANCES

CONSTANTLY LOADING
MISSILES INTO
ROCKET LAUNCHERS

ADDITIONAL TROOPS

MOLOTOV
COCKTAILS

CIVIL UNREST

DODGING SNIPERS

TOO MANY MINE FIELDS

Daily Gripes
Beverly Hills Residents

→ LACK OF PARKING

→ MAINTAINING FIRM BREASTS

→ BEING SEEN IN A HONDA ACCORD

→ AIR POLLUTION

→ TOO MANY AMBULANCE CHASERS

→ CONSTANTLY LOADING SHOPPING BAGS INTO MERCEDES

→ ADDITIONAL TAXES

→ WATERED-DOWN COCKTAILS

→ CIVIL LAWSUITS

→ DODGING VIPERS

→ NOT ENOUGH MRS. FIELDS

Concerns
New Yorkers

GETTING A PARKING SPACE

THE AMOUNT OF SNOW
YOU NEED TO SHOVEL

LIVING ON A NOISY STREET

CONSTANT ROOF LEAKS

GETTING TO GAME EARLY ENOUGH

TOO MUCH SALT ON ROADS

SUCCESS OF PRO SPORTS TEAMS

COST OF LIVING

HIGHS AND LOWS
OF THE STOCK MARKET

BAD WEATHER DAYS

NON-ENGLISH SPEAKING
CAB DRIVERS

Concerns

Los Angelenos

→ GETTING AN AGENT

→ THE AMOUNT OF BULL
YOU NEED TO SHOVEL

→ LIVING ON A FAULT LINE

→ CONSTANT SILICONE LEAKS

→ LEAVING GAME EARLY ENOUGH

→ TOO MUCH SALT ON MARGARITAS

→ SUCCESS OF PLASTIC SURGERY

→ COST OF THERAPY

→ HIGHS AND LOWS
OF THE TIDE

→ BAD HAIR DAYS

→ NON-ENGLISH SPEAKING
7-ELEVEN CLERKS

Family Characteristics
Irish

DRINKING RUNS
IN THE FAMILY

ALWAYS ON
THE SAUCE

ABUNDANCE OF FRECKLES

KNOWN TO FREQUENT THE
NEIGHBORHOOD BARS

YOU CAN'T REFUSE
THEIR BEERS

RELATIVES
BECOME COPS

NICKNAMES LIKE JACK,
WILLIE, PATTI AND HAPPY

Family Characteristics
Italians

→ BURYING BODIES RUNS IN THE FAMILY

→ MAKES A GREAT TOMATO SAUCE

→ ABUNDANCE OF HAIR

→ FREQUENTLY BEING PUT BEHIND BARS

→ YOU CAN'T REFUSE THEIR OFFERS

→ MANY RELATIVES WHO OWN THE COPS

→ NICKNAMES LIKE THE CHIN, THE BULL, THE WEASEL, AND NO-NECK

Bumper Stickers

Democrats

> *My Child Is An Honor Student At*
> **KENNEDY MIDDLE SCHOOL**

> Save The Rain Forest

> THEY CONTROL CONGRESS
> BUT <u>WE</u> CONTROL HOLLYWOOD

> GOT SOCIAL SECURITY?

> SAY **NO** TO FUR!

Bumper Stickers
Republicans

> *My Child Is*
> **WHITE AND WEALTHY!**

> **SAVE THE AUTOMATIC ASSAULT WEAPON**

> WHAT DO YOU EXPECT?
> THEIR LOGO IS A JACK-ASS!

> GOT BULLETS?

> SAY **YES** TO "THE CHAIR"

Favorite Pick-Up Lines
WHITE COLLAR

"YOU CAN SEE THE ENTIRE COASTLINE FROM MY BALCONY."

"I GOT THIS ROLEX FOR BEING THE TOP SALES REP IN THE REGION."

"I ONLY USE THE JAGUAR FOR WEEKEND GETAWAYS."

"I HAPPEN TO BE A GOOD FRIEND OF STEVEN SPIELBERG."

"I HAVE FRONT ROW TICKETS TO THE ELTON JOHN CONCERT."

Favorite Pick-Up Lines
White Trash

"YOU CAN SEE THE K-MART FROM MY BATHROOM WINDOW."

"I GOT THIS TATTOO AFTER I DRANK A CASE OF COORS."

"I ONLY USE THE TRUCK WHEN ITS NOT HITCHED UP TO MY HOUSE."

"MY SECOND WIFE WAS ON THE JERRY SPRINGER SHOW...TWICE!"

"I GOT RINGSIDE SEATS TO THE STONE-COLD STEVE AUSTIN DEATH MATCH."

High Crimes And Misdemeanors
WHITE COLLAR

CHEATING ON SPOUSE

EMBEZZLEMENT

INSIDER TRADING

FORGERY

TAX FRAUD

WRITING BAD CHECKS

BRIBING A JUDGE

CHEATING ON SAT EXAM

High Crimes And Misdemeanors
White Trash

→ **CHEATING ON SIBLING**

→ **SHOPLIFTING FROM THE CIRCLE K**

→ **OUTSIDE URINATING**

→ **FORNICATING WITH SHEEP**

→ **TAXIDERMY FRAUD**

→ **RIDING STOLEN HORSES**

→ **PUNCHING A COP**

→ **CHEATING ON GUN PERMIT TEST**

Questions For An Alien
WHITE COLLAR

WHAT GALAXY ARE YOU FROM?

WHAT IS THE PURPOSE OF YOUR VISIT?

HOW OLD IS YOUR CIVILIZATION?

HOW DO YOU COMMUNICATE?

ARE THERE OTHER FORMS OF LIFE ON YOUR PLANET?

WHAT NUTRIENTS DO YOU NEED TO SURVIVE?

WHAT IS THE ATMOSPHERE MADE UP OF WHERE YOU COME FROM?

Questions For An Alien
White Trash

YOU EVER SEE THAT E.T. GUY?

WHAT KIND OF HORSEPOWER YOU GOT IN THAT SPACESHIP OF YOURS?

HOW DO YOU DRINK BEER WITH NO MOUTH?

YOU GOT ONE OF THEM RAY GUNS I CAN TAKE A FEW SHOTS WITH?

I SEEN STAR WARS 18 TIMES. HOW MANY TIMES YOU SEEN IT?

HOW MANY COUNTRY/WESTERN STATIONS DO YOU PICK UP WITH THAT ANTENNA?

YER NOT GONNA EAT ME, ARE YA?

Anniversary Gifts For Wife
WHITE COLLAR

LOVE LETTER	*Paper*
OAK JEWELRY BOX	*Wood*
TIN MUSIC BOX	*Tin*
BRONZED PHOTO ALBUM	*Bronze*
ELEGANT DINNERWARE	*China*
STERLING SILVER BRACELET	*Silver*
PIANO	*Ivory*
PEARL NECKLACE	*Pearl*
GOLD WATCH	*Gold*

Anniversary Gifts For Wife
White Trash

Paper	**ROLL OF TOILET PAPER**
Wood	**CORD OF FIREWOOD**
Tin	**HUB CAP FROM '78 CAMARO**
Bronze	**BATHROOM PIPING**
China	**BOWLING BALL MADE IN CHINA**
Silver	**FISHING TACKLE**
Ivory	**BAR OF SOAP**
Pearl	**PEARL JAM T-SHIRT**
Gold	**GOLD TOOTH**

Gifts For a Child
WHITE COLLAR

HANDMADE QUILT

STUFFED ANIMAL

PLAY BLOCKS

TEETHING RING

BABY BIB

TICKLE ME ELMO

POGS

FURBY

G.I. JOE

MALIBU BARBIE

BIG WHEEL

Gifts For a Child
White Trash

→ HOMEMADE FIREWORKS

→ A STUFFED OPOSSUM

→ CINDER BLOCKS

→ TOBACCO CHEW

→ BULLETPROOF BIB

→ TICKLE ME EARL

→ COW CHIPS

→ A RACCOON

→ G.I. JETHRO

→ BACKWOODS BOBBIE

→ BIG RADIAL TIRE

Modes Of Communication
WHITE COLLAR

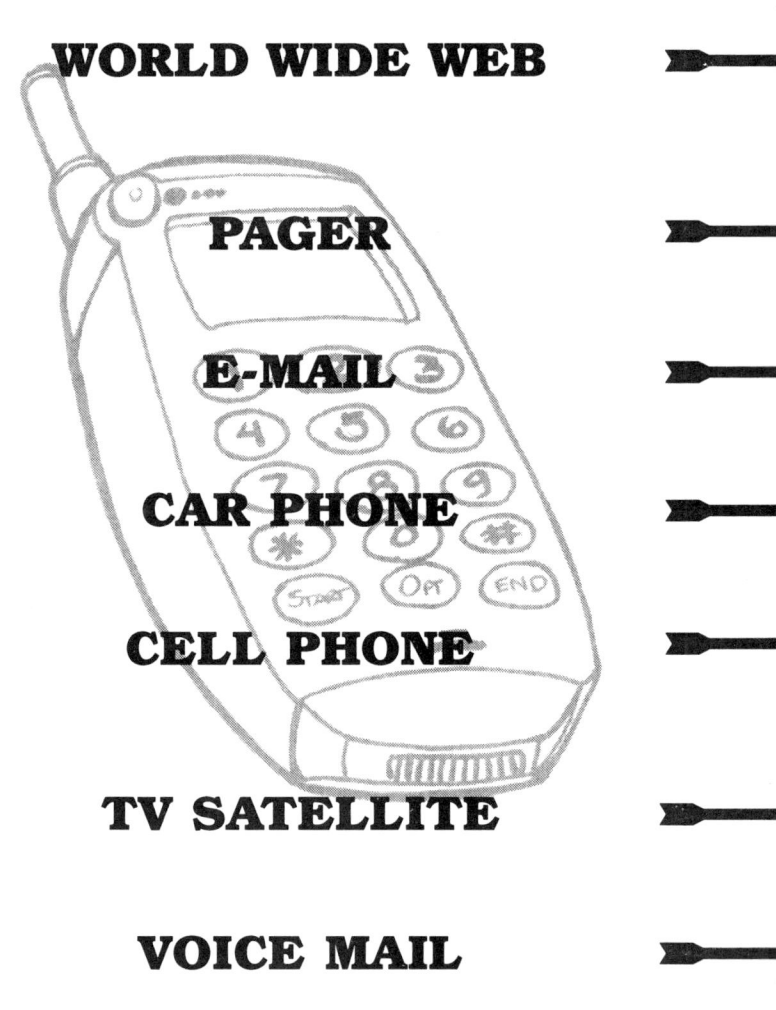

WORLD WIDE WEB

PAGER

E-MAIL

CAR PHONE

CELL PHONE

TV SATELLITE

VOICE MAIL

Modes Of Communication
White Trash

→ **POST OFFICE BULLETIN BOARD**

→ **K-MART INTERCOM**

→ **BULL HORN**

→ **CAR HORN**

→ **TRUCK HORN**

→ **SHOUTING REALLY LOUD OUT WINDOW**

→ **CB RADIO**

Fears
WHITE COLLAR

A BEAR MARKET

TERMITES

RUNNING OUT OF GASOLINE

READING A LETTER FROM THE IRS

SPEAKING IN FRONT OF A
LARGE GROUP OF PEOPLE

GETTING ROBBED
AT GUNPOINT

INABILITY TO MAINTAIN AN ERECTION

GETTING CAUGHT CHEATING
WITH YOUR SECRETARY

RUNNING OUT OF VIAGRA
BEFORE A BIG DATE

TAKING AN HIV BLOOD TEST

CABLE GOES OUT
DURING SUPERBOWL

Fears
White Trash

→ A BEAR IN YOUR HOUSE

→ TORNADOES

→ RUNNING OUT OF MIRACLE WHIP

→ READING

→ SPEAKING IN FRONT OF A PAROLE BOARD

→ GETTING CAUGHT ROBBING SOMEONE AT GUNPOINT

→ INABILITY TO KILL A SLOW ANIMAL.

→ GETTING CAUGHT CHEATING WITH YOUR SISTER

→ RUNNING OUT OF AMMUNITION BEFORE A KLAN MEETING

→ TAKING A TEST

→ CABLE GOES OUT DURING MONSTER TRUCK SHOW

Ian Cohen

Although a Los Angeles native, Ian attended Ithaca College in upstate New York where he graduated with a degree and frostbite. Immediately putting his education to work, he moved to Orlando Florida and accepted a highly challenging position with the Disney Corporation. You may recognize him as the guy in the purple polyester jump suit who said, "Watch your step," as you boarded your ride. Against all good judgment, Ian left his promising Disney career to seek even greater opportunities back in Los Angeles. His first comedy-writing stint included such memorable lines as "Congratulations, you may be our next million dollar winner." It wasn't until several years later that he was lured over to DreamWorks Television by Steven Spielberg (or at least some guy who worked for him) to write for the wildly popular, three-month hit show, "Majority Rules." From there, he used what little knowledge of women he had, to become the only male heterosexual writer for Lifetime TV's all-girl game show, "Who Knows You Best?"

Ian currently resides in Woodland Hills, California with his dog Magic.

Sean Collins

Sean Collins, born in Manhattan and raised in the Bronx, now resides in Los Angeles, California. He was educated at New York University, where he continues to pay off enormous student loans.

Sean's life experiences include the following: bartender (who drank more than he poured), actor, comedian, Brazilian-style Jiu Jitsu fighter (who has actually never been to Brazil), freelance magazine writer, personal fitness trainer (who at times...got too personal), creative director for a sweepstakes company (a guy who regrettably wrote "You definitely may have won $3 million!"), and "Wall Street" consultant to numerous publicly held companies in the Internet, medical, retail, high-technology, and entertainment sectors.

A true humanitarian and animal lover, Sean favors foreplay over football...except during playoff season. Sean's life-long dream is revealed under the category "3 Granted Wishes" on page 21.

TITLES BY CCC PUBLICATIONS

Blank Books ($3.99)
GUIDE TO SEX AFTER BABY
GUIDE TO SEX AFTER 30
GUIDE TO SEX AFTER 40
GUIDE TO SEX AFTER 50
GUIDE TO SEX AFTER MARRIAGE

Retail $4.95 – $4.99
"?" book
LAST DIET BOOK YOU'LL EVER NEED
CAN SEX IMPROVE YOUR GOLF?
THE COMPLETE BOOGER BOOK
FLYING FUNNIES
MARITAL BLISS & OXYMORONS
THE ADULT DOT-TO-DOT BOOK
THE DEFINITIVE FART BOOK
THE COMPLETE WIMP'S GUIDE TO SEX
THE CAT OWNER'S SHAPE UP MANUAL
THE OFFICE FROM HELL
FITNESS FANATICS
YOUNGER MEN ARE BETTER THAN RETIN-A
BUT OSSIFER, IT'S NOT MY FAULT
YOU KNOW YOU'RE AN OLD FART WHEN...
1001 WAYS TO PROCRASTINATE
HORMONES FROM HELL II
SHARING THE ROAD WITH IDIOTS
THE GREATEST ANSWERING MACHINE MESSAGES
WHAT DO WE DO NOW??
HOW TO TALK YOU WAY OUT OF A TRAFFIC TICKET
THE BOTTOM HALF
LIFE'S MOST EMBARRASSING MOMENTS
HOW TO ENTERTAIN PEOPLE YOU HATE
YOUR GUIDE TO CORPORATE SURVIVAL
NO HANG-UPS (Volumes I, II & III – $3.95 ea.)
TOTALLY OUTRAGEOUS BUMPER-SNICKERS ($2.95)

Retail $5.95
30 – DEAL WITH IT!
40 – DEAL WITH IT!
50 – DEAL WITH IT!
60 – DEAL WITH IT!
OVER THE HILL – DEAL WITH IT!
SLICK EXCUSES FOR STUPID SCREW-UPS
SINGLE WOMEN VS. MARRIED WOMEN
TAKE A WOMAN'S WORD FOR IT
SEXY CROSSWORD PUZZLES
SO, YOU'RE GETTING MARRIED
YOU KNOW HE'S A WOMANIZING SLIMEBALL WHEN...
GETTING OLD SUCKS
WHY GOD MAKES BALD GUYS
OH BABY!
PMS CRAZED: TOUCH ME AND I'LL KILL YOU!
WHY MEN ARE CLUELESS
THE BOOK OF WHITE TRASH
THE ART OF MOONING
GOLFAHOLICS
CRINKLED 'N' WRINKLED
SMART COMEBACKS FOR STUPID QUESTIONS
YIKES! IT'S ANOTHER BIRTHDAY

SEX IS A GAME
SEX AND YOUR STARS
SIGNS YOUR SEX LIFE IS DEAD
MALE BASHING: WOMEN'S FAVORITE PASTIME
THINGS YOU CAN DO WITH A USELESS MAN
MORE THINGS YOU CAN DO WITH A USELESS MAN
RETIREMENT: THE GET EVEN YEARS
LITTLE INSTRUCTION BOOK OF THE RICH & FAMOUS
WELCOME TO YOUR MIDLIFE CRISIS
GETTING EVEN WITH THE ANSWERING MACHINE
ARE YOU A SPORTS NUT?
MEN ARE PIGS / WOMEN ARE BITCHES
THE BETTER HALF
ARE WE DYSFUNCTIONAL YET?
TECHNOLOGY BYTES!
50 WAYS TO HUSTLE YOUR FRIENDS
HORMONES FROM HELL
HUSBANDS FROM HELL
KILLER BRAS & Other Hazards Of The 50's
IT'S BETTER TO BE OVER THE HILL THAN UNDER IT
HOW TO REALLY PARTY!!!
WORK SUCKS!
THE PEOPLE WATCHER'S FIELD GUIDE
THE ABSOLUTE LAST CHANCE DIET BOOK
THE UGLY TRUTH ABOUT MEN
NEVER A DULL CARD
THE LITTLE BOOK OF ROMANTIC LIES

Retail $6.95
EVERYTHING I KNOW I LEARNED FROM TRASH TALK TV
IN A PERFECT WORLD
I WISH I DIDN'T...
THE TOILET ZONE
SIGNS/TOO MUCH TIME W/CAT
LOVE & MARRIAGE & DIVORCE
CYBERGEEK IS CHIC
THE DIFFERENCE BETWEEN MEN AND WOMEN
GO TO HEALTH!
NOT TONIGHT, DEAR, I HAVE A COMPUTER!
THINGS YOU WILL NEVER HEAR THEM SAY
THE SENIOR CITIZENS'S SURVIVAL GUIDE
IT'S A MAD MAD MAD SPORTS WORLD
THE LITTLE BOOK OF CORPORATE LIES
RED HOT MONOGAMY
LOVE DAT CAT
HOW TO SURVIVE A JEWISH MOTHER

Retail $7.95
WHY MEN DON'T HAVE A CLUE
LADIES, START YOUR ENGINES!
ULI STEIN'S "ANIMAL LIFE"
ULI STEIN'S "I'VE GOT IT BUT IT'S JAMMED"
ULI STEIN'S "THAT SHOULD NEVER HAVE HAPPENED"

NO HANG-UPS – CASSETTES Retail $5.98
Vol. I: GENERAL MESSAGES (M or F)
Vol. II: BUSINESS MESSAGES (M or F)
Vol. III: 'R' RATED MESSAGES (M or F)
Vol. V: CELEBRI-TEASE